SADDLEBACK STABLES

Pony Camp

Written by Lisa Thompson

Illustrated by Molly Sage

Blake
EDUCATION
Better ways to learn

Saddleback Stables: Pony Camp
ISBN: 978 1 76020 164 7

Lexile®Measure: 690L
For more information visit www.lexile.com
Lexile © 2013 MetaMetrics, Inc.

Text copyright © 2018 Lisa Thompson
Written by Lisa Thompson
Illustrations copyright © 2018 Blake Publishing
Illustrated by Molly Sage

Published by Blake Education Pty Ltd
ABN 50 074 266 023
108 Main Road
Clayton South VIC 3169
info@blake.com.au
www.blake.com.au

Publisher: Katy Pike
Series editor: Mark Stafford
Page layout: Modern Art Production Group
Printer: 1010 Printing Asia Limited

CONTENTS

Jordy

Chief

Sophie

Peaches

Hannah

Jin Jin

Bella

Alexa

Gypsy Rose

Billy Blaze

4

CHAPTER ONE

Camp Hiccup

Hannah skipped up the road to Saddleback Stables, swinging her overnight bag. It was Pony Camp weekend! Hannah and her riding friends would have **two full days** of riding fun and stay at the stables overnight. They had been looking forward to it for months.

Hannah spotted Sophie leading Peaches, the palomino pony, into the stables. Hannah ran to catch up with them.

"Pony Camp, here we come!" she yelled excitedly. Hannah fell silent when she saw Sophie's long face.

Sophie led Peaches into her stall. Bella sat against the wall on a bale of hay, looking just as gloomy.

"What's wrong?" asked Hannah. "The camp hasn't been cancelled, has it?"

"Not yet," sighed Sophie, **plonking** herself down next to Bella, "but I bet it will be."

"Why? What do you mean?" asked Hannah.

"Jordy can't come because he has to visit his grandparents in the country," explained Bella.

Jordy was in their Saturday riding class as well, and the best rider in their group.

"Lola can't come because she has a tummy bug," added Sophie.

Hannah felt bad about Jordy and Lola but didn't understand why the camp had to be cancelled.

"And now," said Sophie, "Alexa is about to go home because Billy Blaze is **lame** and can't be ridden. Miss Jill says that there needs to be at least four riders for the camp to go ahead."

Sophie pointed to where Miss Jill, the owner of Saddleback Stables, was with Alexa. They were in the paddock with Billy Blaze, who stood with one hoof slightly off the ground.

"If Alexa goes home, we all go," moaned Sophie.

"And we all know Alexa only rides Billy Blaze," said Bella. "It means the camp's over before it even started."

Hannah sank down next to her friends. Disappointment **washed** over her. She knew how seriously Alexa took her horseriding and how proud she was of her beautiful thoroughbred, Billy Blaze. "But surely," thought Hannah, "Alexa could ride another pony, just this once?"

Hannah was about to go out and **plead** with Alexa and Miss Jill not to cancel the camp when they both appeared at the stable door.

"Morning, girls," said Miss Jill. She put her arm around Alexa's shoulders and smiled. Alexa frowned and looked at her boots. The girls waited for the bad news.

"As I'm sure you all know," explained Miss Jill, "there needs to be at least four riders for Pony Camp to go ahead. Poor Billy Blaze has come up lame this morning. Nothing serious, thank goodness, but he does need rest for a couple of days."

Sophie huffed with disappointment.

"But," continued Miss Jill, "Alexa has kindly agreed to ride Oscar, one of the stable ponies."

"Really?" cried Sophie, **leaping** up and **wrapping** Alexa in a hug. "Thanks Alexa!"

Alexa remained silent, her arms frozen to her sides.

"Yeah thanks, Alexa," said Bella. "That's awesome." She glanced at Hannah with a look of surprise.

Hannah smiled her thanks to Alexa but Alexa looked away.

"My niece, Riya, will lead this year's camp," explained Miss Jill. "She's on her university holidays. When she was your age, Riya went to every pony camp in the district. She's seen them all and has lots of fun things planned for you. It'll be more relaxed than our Saturday lessons but you'll still learn a lot. Camp is a great time to get to know your ponies better."

Alexa **scowled** when she heard this.

"Right then," said Miss Jill, sounding pleased and relieved. "I'll leave you to get your ponies ready. Riya will meet you in the main arena."

"Thanks for letting the camp go ahead, Alexa," said Hannah when Miss Jill had gone. "I know you only like to ride Billy Blaze, but Oscar is a really good pony. You two will have fun."

"Oscar is a stable pony," **huffed** Alexa. "You can't seriously compare him to Billy Blaze."

"Anyway, it's great you're staying," said Sophie. "I totally expected the camp to be cancelled. I'm so glad it's not."

Alexa folded her arms. "It might still be. I'm not promising anything. I'll stay as long as I can stand it." She rolled her eyes. "I can't believe I agreed to ride Oscar. Camp can go ahead for now, but if I want to go home I will. What could that tired old stable pony do that Billy Blaze hasn't done a hundred times before, and better?"

Alexa **stormed** off to the tack room.

"She'll be fine once we're all riding," said Hannah. "She's just worried about Billy Blaze."

"You think?" said Bella. "I'm not so sure. I bet Alexa finds plenty of reasons to go home the moment she gets on Oscar."

CHAPTER TWO

Riya Says

Riya wore blue jodhpurs, a Saddleback Stables shirt and short brown riding boots. Her long hair hung in a single plait down her back. Her horse was a beautiful chestnut mare with **white socks** and a **small star** on her forehead. She stood calm and proud.

The girls and their ponies made a line in front of Riya in the centre of the arena. Riya's smile put everyone at ease—except Alexa, who entered the arena sulkily on Oscar and did her best to ignore everyone.

Hannah rode Jin Jin, a skewbald pony. Like Oscar, he belonged to the stables. Sophie rode Peaches, and Bella was on Gypsy Rose, a strawberry roan pony.

Standing a little way from the others, Alexa tried to get Oscar into line. He moved this way and that, **refusing** to line up with the other ponies. It took three attempts for Alexa to get him in position.

"Welcome to Saddleback Stables Pony Camp," Riya said cheerfully. "I hope you have as much fun this weekend as I did at pony camp. Camp is a great way to learn about and **bond** with your pony, and of course with your riding friends. Before we start, tell me a bit about yourself and your pony. I'll go first. My name is Riya and this is my horse, Mindy. I've had her for three years. She's a quick learner, loves jumping and is a great trail horse."

Riya nodded at Hannah to go next.

"My name is Hannah Harrison and this is Jin Jin. I've been riding him for about eight months. He's also a quick learner and doesn't mind competing. He's a bit cheeky but very clever."

Jin Jin's ears flicked and he **Snorted**, to say he agreed with everything Hannah said.

Sophie was next. "Hi, I'm Sophie Chen and this is Peaches. She's kind and gives most things a go, a bit like me, I guess. She is very trusting and loves trail riding and even some jumping."

Sophie looked at Bella. "I'm Bella and

this is my pony, Gypsy Rose. I think she's gentle but playful. She used to be afraid of the water down at the creek but not anymore, thanks to Jin Jin and lots of visits there. Now it's one of her **favourite places**."

"Good to hear," said Riya. "We'll go down to Cockatoo Creek later today."

The girls looked at Alexa, waiting for her to introduce herself, but she said nothing.

"What about you, Miss Lucky Last?" said Riya.

Hannah winced when Riya said "last". Alexa didn't like to be last at anything.

"My name is Alexa MacKenzie," said Alexa finally, straightening herself in the saddle. "This is Oscar. He belongs to Saddleback Stables. I have never ridden him before. I only ever ride my own horse, but he's lame at the moment." Alexa **Sighed** and looked down at her saddle. "If I had to describe Oscar in a few words, I would say he's slow, scruffy and stubborn."

Oscar flicked his head and stomped the ground. He understood he had just been insulted.

"I see," said Riya. "Well, I don't know if all that's true. Oscar used to be *my* pony. He's actually very smart. He's also fast and strong. I won quite a few ribbons at pony club events riding him."

Alexa raised an eyebrow. Riya **dismounted** and tied Mindy up to the rail of the arena. She walked back to the girls.

"I'll quickly check your gear before we start, so both you and your pony are comfortable. We'll start with you, Alexa. Be extra careful when tacking up a new pony. You don't know their habits as well as your regular pony." Riya lengthened Alexa's stirrups by a notch and gave Oscar a pat. "I think you two

20

are going to learn a lot from each other."

Riya turned to check Gypsy Rose and didn't see Alexa frown. Hannah smiled at Alexa, hoping to make her feel better, but Alexa looked away.

After Riya finished checking the ponies, she mounted Mindy again and rode to the centre of the arena.

"Okay, let's start with a game of 'Riya Says'. Warm up with a walk around the arena, keeping some distance between each other. When I say so, change your pony's gait from **walk to trot or canter**. This game is all about rhythm and keeping your seat. Think about how you're sitting in the saddle and maintaining a rhythm with your pony."

Hannah noticed Oscar move closer to Peaches. Peaches didn't like being crowded and she kicked out to let Oscar know.

"Pull him up, Alexa," said Riya. "Let him know he's not going first. Oscar can be a little bossy."

"A bit like his rider," said Bella quietly to Hannah as they began their walk.

Alexa pulled the reins, but Oscar tossed his head to get them back. He glared at her but slowed his walk. Alexa worked hard to get him to fall into line between Jin Jin and Gypsy Rose.

"Riya says trot!" yelled Riya.

The girls **tapped** their ponies into a trot. Hannah concentrated on finding her rhythm—up, down, up, down. Once she found it, she looked around the arena. Alexa, who always rode so smoothly on Billy Blaze, was bouncing around on Oscar **like a beginner**. Oscar's trot was a jumble of hooves and jolts.

"Riya says canter!" yelled Riya.

The riders urged their ponies on and they broke into a canter—except for Oscar, who was now trotting properly

but slowly. Alexa gave him a short, sharp kick.

"Come on, Oscar boy," called Riya. "Relax with him, Alexa. Work together, not against each other."

Hannah could see how unhappy Alexa was at being told how to ride.

Riya called the riders back to a trot, another canter, a trot and finally a walk. Hannah was pleased at how well she and Jin Jin had ridden. "Good work," she said softly and rubbed his neck. Jin Jin nickered happily.

Everyone looked happy, except for Alexa and Oscar. Alexa **glowered** at the ground. Oscar bobbed his head and **chomped** on his bit.

"Nice work, girls," grinned Riya. "That

was just a warm-up. Now we're going to ride without stirrups."

Hannah felt butterflies stir in her belly.

"I've never done that before," said Sophie nervously.

"I do it all the time with Billy Blaze," declared Alexa, slipping her boots out of her stirrups.

"Pony camp is the place to try new things," said Riya **reassuringly**. "Take your feet out of the stirrups and cross the stirrups up over the front of the saddle." She lifted Mindy's stirrups and crossed them neatly either side of her pommel. The girls did the same.

"Now, remember your seat for balance," continued Riya. "If you feel wobbly, grab the pommel. Keep hold of the reins. Alright, Riya says … walk!" The girls nudged the ponies into a walk. "Grip your pony with your thighs and knees. **Not too tight**. Yes, that's good. Riya says trot!"

The girls **bounced** about without their stirrups to steady them. Bella grasped Gypsy Rose's pommel and went up and down smoothly.

"Riya says canter!"

Hannah gulped. How could she canter without stirrups and remain on Jin Jin? But Hannah remembered the rhythm of a canter is much smoother than a trot. She didn't fall off, and as Riya asked them to walk, trot and canter again, Hannah grew in confidence.

Hannah again glanced across at Alexa. This time she looked bored. She even yawned.

"I think that's enough for now," said Riya finally. "Come back into the middle. Put your stirrups down and line up."

Alexa and Oscar lined up next to Hannah and Jin Jin. "Thank goodness that's over," mumbled Alexa.

"Please take your ponies back to the stables," said Riya, "and give them a rub down. I'll meet you there in a minute."

Sophie led the girls out of the arena. "My bottom hurts from all that bouncing," she said, laughing.

"Mine too, and my thighs," added Bella. "That was hard work!"

"Sure was," said Hannah, "but fun, especially the cantering." Hannah looked over her shoulder to check on Alexa. Alexa sat **glumly** on Oscar as they walked slowly along. "Hey, Alexa, ride up and join us," she called.

Alexa shook her head.

"She's **sulking**," said Bella.

"At least she's still here," said Sophie.

28

Back at the stables, Alexa quickly unsaddled Oscar, put him in a stall and headed for the door.

"Hey, where are you going?" asked Hannah.

"To check on Billy Blaze," replied Alexa, without stopping.

"But what about Oscar?" asked Sophie. "You're meant to look after him."

Alexa kept walking.

CHAPTER THREE

Friendly Advice

"Where's Alexa?" asked Riya as she entered the stables.

"She's gone to check on Billy Blaze," said Bella. "We can give Oscar a rub down."

"I know you can," said Riya, "but that's Alexa's job. She's riding him, so she's responsible for him."

"I'm sure she won't be long," said Hannah quickly. "I'll go get her."

"Thanks Hannah, that would be great," said Riya. "While you're gone, I'm going to check with Aunt Jill about what I've got planned next."

Hannah **jogged** over to Billy Blaze's paddock. She found Alexa sitting on the fence, watching her horse **nibble** grass.

"Hey, Alexa, Riya wants you to come back to the stables and look after Oscar."

"Can't you tell her I'm busy?"

Hannah climbed the fence and sat next to Alexa.

"You know, watching Billy Blaze won't make him heal quicker." Alexa said nothing. "Sophie and Bella are rubbing Oscar down for you." Alexa nodded.

Hannah took a **deep breath**. "We were all really looking forward to pony camp, Alexa. And we're happy you're riding Oscar, so camp is still on. But it would be better if *you* were happy about it. It just feels like camp could still be cancelled because you decide to go home."

Hannah waited for Alexa to explode and say camp was definitely cancelled. Instead, Alexa **bit her lip** and then mumbled, "I know … I just … well, I only like riding Billy Blaze."

"That's because you *only* ride Billy Blaze," Hannah said as calmly as she could. "You haven't given Oscar a chance. Think of it like this. Billy Blaze is your best pony friend, right?" Alexa nodded. "Well, it's okay to have other pony friends. I think you're afraid to ride Oscar because you're so loyal to Billy Blaze. And maybe you think Oscar isn't good enough for you."

"No, I don't want to ride Oscar because he's slow and stubborn and shaggy," snapped Alexa. "What is there to like about riding him? Look at him!"

"Riya doesn't think he's slow and stubborn. And maybe Oscar can do things that Billy Blaze can't … if you give him a go."

"What could they possibly be?" asked Alexa, folding her arms.

"There are a lot of ponies here, Alexa. Miss Jill wouldn't have picked Oscar for you, out of all the ponies at Saddleback Stables, unless there was something you could learn from him."

Alexa was quiet for a moment. "That might be true," she said.

"You know it is. But you have to give Oscar a proper chance."

Alexa took a deep breath. She sat up straighter on the fence. "Are Sophie and Bella upset with me?"

"A little. But they won't be if you stay and try to have a good time. We all just want to enjoy the camp. Look, Alexa, we might not always get along but we're all friends."

Alexa jumped down off the fence. She smiled at Hannah.

"Okay, I'll do it. I'll give Oscar a chance." She turned towards the paddock. "See you later, Billy Blaze!"

Billy Blaze **whinnied** goodbye as the girls ran back to the stables.

37

CHAPTER FOUR

Back to Basics

Riya gathered the riders around her. "Now that everyone is here," she said, "lead your ponies up to the top paddock. You'll just need a halter."

"No saddle?" asked Sophie.

"No saddle," replied Riya.

"Will we ride bareback?" asked Bella excitedly.

Riya nodded. "You sure will. Riding without stirrups was your warm-up."

"Woo-hoo!" cried Bella and **high-fived** Sophie. "I love bareback riding!"

Hannah had never ridden bareback

before. She felt her butterflies stir again. She looked at Alexa, expecting her to be as excited as the others, but she was frowning again. Rather than unhappy or bored, Alexa looked worried.

Hannah **jogged** up beside Riya as she led Jin Jin. "I've never ridden bareback, Riya," she confessed.

"Me neither," added Alexa. "When I got Billy Blaze, his last owner said he didn't like it, so I never tried."

"It's true that some ponies don't like being ridden bareback," said Riya, "but you'll be fine with Jin Jin and Oscar. Their shaggy coats will make it easier to hold on. I used to have so much fun riding Oscar bareback. It's a lot different to riding in a saddle. The more you relax, the easier it is to move with your pony." Riya ran ahead to help Bella and Sophie with the gate.

Alexa raised an eyebrow at Hannah. "Maybe this is why Miss Jill gave me Oscar to ride. He's good at bareback riding and she knew I'd never tried it before. I guess I'm about to find out."

"We all are," said Hannah with a nervous giggle.

Gypsy Rose was used to Bella riding without a saddle. Riya held the reins while Bella **vaulted** onto her pony. The others mounted, one by one, by **stepping** onto an upturned bucket.

"Just let your legs hang," said Riya. "If you grip with your legs, your pony will think you want to go faster. Relax, get

comfortable and move as your pony moves. Get a feel for each other. We'll start with walking."

Hannah quickly realised everything was different. Without the saddle for balance, she slid over Jin Jin's back as he walked. Hannah **focused** on staying relaxed. She held the reins firmly and threaded her fingers through Jin Jin's shaggy mane to steady herself.

Hannah looked over at Alexa. She seemed completely at ease on Oscar as they walked and trotted. They were no longer battling each other.

"I want to canter," Alexa said eagerly.

"Let's just stay with walking and trotting for now," Riya advised. "Take your time, at your own pace."

Then without warning, Alexa and Oscar broke into a canter and **swept** past everyone.

"Wooooooo-hooooo!" she cried, as she and Oscar flew across the paddock. As they neared the fence on the far side of the paddock, they slowed to a trot and then a walk. Alexa leaned forward and patted Oscar, and he gave a **wild whinny**.

"I was so wrong about him!" Alexa called across the paddock. "Oscar isn't slow at all!"

Sophie and Bella were soon cantering too. Hannah took her time. She bounced and slid when Jin Jin trotted, which made her nervous about going any faster. But she could feel Jin Jin wanting to run like the other ponies, so she gave him a nudge and he broke forward. As soon as Jin Jin changed

Wooooo-hoooo!

gait, Hannah slipped into the smooth rhythm of the canter. She relaxed and raced across the paddock to join the others.

"Well done," said Alexa. "You were right—I just needed to give Oscar a chance. He's a **great little pony**. You wouldn't know it to look at him though."

"So you're staying at camp?" asked Sophie.

Alexa nodded. "I'm sorry about before."

"That's okay," said Bella. "Just don't change your mind."

"I won't," said Alexa firmly. "Who knows what other things Oscar could teach me."

"There'll be more time for bareback later," Riya said. "Now it's time for lunch. Let's pack our lunches and ride to Cockatoo Creek."

"Yes to that!" said Bella.

The girls followed Riya down to the stables, **chatting** and **giggling** on their ponies, eager for the fun and surprises that can only be had at pony camp.

PONY PROFILE

Name: Billy Blaze

Age: 5

Rider: Alexa MacKenzie

Owner: Alexa MacKenzie

Breed: Thoroughbred

Height: 14.5 hands (a small horse, rather than a pony)

Temperament: responsive, learns quickly and likes to lead. He can be flighty unless ridden by an experienced rider.

Coat: dark bay (brown coat with black mane and tail)

Markings: white blaze, black stockings

Habits: likes to lead, pick up the pace, and show how beautifully he can move and jump

Likes: dressage, showjumping, performing and winning

Dislikes: mud, trail rides, and being ridden by anyone other than Alexa

Did you know? Thoroughbreds are popular for their speed, focus and elegance. They are bred for racing and love to gallop. Thoroughbreds are also great at dressage, showjumping and other competitions.

GLOSSARY

bit
a piece of metal put in a pony's mouth to allow a rider to control it

gait
the way a pony moves: walk, trot, canter or gallop

halter
a rope or strap for leading a horse or pony

jodhpurs
full-length riding pants

lame
not able to walk due to a foot or leg injury

mare
an adult female horse